Shane Darke is a psychologist and Professor at the National Drug & Alcohol Research Centre (University of New South Wales). He is one of the world's leading researchers in drug and alcohol, has written three academic books, and published more than 270 scientific articles. He is a lover of absurdist comedy, including *The Goons*, Douglas Adams, Stanislaw Lem and *Red Dwarf*. Shane lives in Sydney, Australia.

TALES FROM THE SOCIETY FOR THE PRESERVATION OF PREPOSTEROUS ABSURDITY

Shane Darke

First published by Critical Mass in 2019
This edition published in 2019 by Critical Mass

Copyright © Shane Darke 2019

The moral right of the author has been asserted.

All rights reserved. This publication (or any part of it) may not be reproduced or transmitted, copied, stored, distributed or otherwise made available by any person or entity (including Google, Amazon or similar organisations), in any form (electronic, digital, optical, mechanical) or by any means (photocopying, recording, scanning or otherwise) without prior written permission from the publisher.

Tales from the Society for the Preservation of Preposterous Absurdity

EPUB: 9781925786446
POD: 9781925786453

Cover design by Red Tally Studios

Publishing services provided by Critical Mass
www.critmassconsulting.com

To Skye, Jessica and Lilly. Absurdists all.

Preface

The Society for the Preservation of Preposterous Absurdity was founded in 1453, by Sir Snedley Sniverington. Born in the Bronze Age, Sir Snedley fought at Troy (on both sides), the Peloponnesian Wars (on both sides) and the Crusades (on three sides). For this excellent all-round service, he was knighted by the Fellowship for the Salvation of the Unknown Universe.

Upon the Fall of Byzantium, it was evident to Sir Snedley that absurdity, or more specifically, *preposterous* absurdity, had become a threat unto the multiverse, and even to its very self. Indeed, things had come to a pretty pass when a perfectly respectable Roman Empire could not be Greek and a slightly less respectable Greek Empire could not be

Roman. He commented 'Preposterous absurdity is *strong* meat. Dangerous to those who do not know how to handle the beast. We need to preserve preposterous absurdity *for* the world, and preserve the world *from* preposterous absurdity.' Strong, wise words. Sir Snedley's vision was for a learned society to wield this double-edged sword safely, and to preserve it for preposterity. He set up office in a prime residence, number 13, on Great Snarkley Street, where the Society resides to this day.

After the untimely death of Sir Snedley early in his fourth millennium, in circumstances detailed in this tome, the role of Society President fell to your humble scribe. I had worked at the Society for some centuries, having risen from the rank of Guttersnipe 3rd Class, to the highly sought-after Muckraker 1st Class, and thence to Vice-President. Shortly after his death, Sir Snedley remarked, 'Smotheringale, you are the most absurd person I know, and the third most absurd person I have never heard of. You were born for the job.' Needless to say, I was humbled by such high praise.

Having now learnt the Society's ropes, I feel it's time to put them away in a safe place and pick up the quill. Noting a lack of historical documentation (due to Sir Snedley's humility and lack of loquaciousness), I seek to record the works of the Society, so as to inform the multiverse of our noble endeavours, for its bafflement and edification. We in the Society deal with events well beyond the experience of the average citizen, so in these tales the reader may come across unfamiliar terms. If such is the case, the reader is referred to the Glossary, compiled by the Society for the linguistic enrichment of all sentient, and non-sentient, beings.

In our works, which are legion, we are guided always by the motto of our founder: *Here to help, hope to hinder.*

Dr Martin Smotheringale

President

The Society for the Preservation of Preposterous Absurdity

The Wave Surfer

It was a rare quiet day at the Society office. I had screwed in both my monocles so I could more fully focus on the absence of events. My God, the ennui was so existential that it had burnt the paint. At least this is better than watching it dry, I mused, finding some solace. And I speak from experience, having sat through the Great Paint Drying of 1763. I idly scanned my nameplate: Dr Martin Smotheringale, Society President. 'A somewhat pedestrian name for a man in such an important position,' I thought aloud, rather stridently, to an obviously astonished chair.

I ran a fatherly eye over the various Society treasures, placed to impress the impressionable and for us to remember the rememberable: the Great

One-Legged Rhinoceros of Rockingham, the Perpetual Irritation Machine, the Hypercube and, of course, Schrödinger's Catbox. I had a vague yearning to open the latter, but that would mean paying for a funeral, cat food, or both. The Society's funds do not run to such conspicuous largesse.

It was at this morbidinous moment that he appeared. Now, when I say appeared, I mean to say *appeared*. One instant he was not, and then he was. No in-between. This was a real pity, as I do rather like in-betweens. They comfort me. I raised a quizzical eyebrow that I kept handy for such occasions and adjusted my monocles, the better to observe this astonishing apparition. He was dressed alarmingly, though with élan, in patent bronze moccasins, lightweight concrete trousers, and a Tyrolean hat with a rather jaunty dinosaur feather. His age was indeterminate. I felt certain, however, that he was either nineteen or ninety-one.

He looked at me with eyes of sorrow, as so many seem to do, and spoke. 'Dr Smotheringale, I am afraid that I find myself in a rather preposterous situation with, it must be said, certain elements of absurdity. I have sought help from the usual fly-by-night institutions – Harvard, Cambridge, the Sorbonne. Good God, sir, even Oxford! They know nothing. Nothing, sir. In this reality at least, the wisdom of your respected Society appears to be my only hope. Sir, I am desperate.'

'My good man, I am sorry you wasted your time amongst such charlatans. I may say confidently, that if we cannot help, we may at least hinder. Now, like every good story, let us start at the end.'

'Dr Smotheringale, my name is Sebastian Snorgle. I am a wave surfer. The best. Indeed, the only.'

'Not in those trousers, surely?' I observed, archly.

'A *quantum* wave surfer, Dr Smotheringale. No water involved. As a man of your conspicuous erudition would know, all reality is just a collection of probability waves. And I can see them. I can find the right wave, no matter how improbable, and ride it in to reality. By the way, do you, by any chance, have a cat in that box?'

'Yes and no. Please continue.' Fearing that this could be a long tale, I lit a two-metre cheroot I carried in my pocket.

'It started innocently enough. Stacking an infinite number of aardvarks nose to tail, tossing heads 37,123 times in a row. Using real heads. The usual adolescent pranks. Then it started to get out of hand. My unconscious mind started to shape reality. I only had to think of something absurd, and *there* it was. I mean, there I was thinking of concrete trousers, as we all do from time to time' – I knew all too well – 'and, well, there they were. Nicely tailored, lightweight and rather comfortable, but they do not seem to want to go away. I do also rather like the bronze moccasins.' They were, indeed, excellent.

Sebastian continued, 'Then, of course, there was the Mars Incident. I had idly mused that I had half a mind to go to Mars. And there I was. Well, not all. Only the front half. Most unsettling. And cold. My mind was sluggish, the back half being ensconced back on Earth. In any case, fortunately my back half was so affronted by its frontlessness that it willed me back at once, leaving two half-footprints on Mars. Two small half-steps for mankind. By this time, my decoherence was out of control. Every obscure probability vied for my attention to become reality. I am a threat to myself, sir. Indeed, I am a threat to the entire cosmos!'

Hmm, this could not continue. His decoherence was accelerating rapidly. Every random thought was likely to spring into the cosmos and parade its probabilistic preposterousness. Already, the room was filling rapidly. A talented group of dancing turtles competed for floor space with several of the smaller infinities. A rather angry feathery dinosaur, of modest but robust proportions, leapt into existence, and headed straight for the millinery of my beleaguered guest. Catching the fearsome eye of the Great One-Legged One, a beast not to be trifled with in reality or unreality, he departed our reality for safer, Rhinocerosless climes. Dear God, if the Great One-Legged One was getting involved, this *was* serious. If a complete quantum catastrophe was to be avoided, and my preposterous guest was to be saved, the Society would have to act. The situation clearly called for urgent procrastination.

'Let me think.' I rarely indulge in thought myself, but people say it helps.

Upon moderately sober reflection – a hogshead worth of Liversludge Gin (*'It'll kill you or cure you'*) having suddenly appeared in my bloodstream – I announced, perhaps injudiciously, 'Why, the answer is staring us in the face.' Loose words under the circumstances, for suddenly there the answer itself was, looking at me with a stern and steely eye. Most disconcerting. They are taller than I thought. Averting my eyes from this perplexing phantasm, I continued. 'In any case, it is clear to me that we must take the advice of the sagacious, if mythical, Dr Pangloss, *"All is for the best in the best of all possible worlds"*. The only way to end your quantum decoherence and, it must be said, questionable dress sense, is for you to will the best of all possible worlds. Cohere the waves. Ride them all. No more chaos, no concrete trousers, and Mars may be left to the fully fronted. Eternal peace and satisfaction.'

His eyes lit up like lit-up eyes. 'You're right. Of course! That's the solution. That's just what I'll do.' He glanced around at the maniacal menagerie manoeuvring through the mezzanine and noted, 'This one is a tad tawdry after all.'

'Might I, perchance, come too?' I enquired. I must say, it did sound rather good. At least for a while. It certainly had to be quieter than my office, a brass band of monkeys having launched into a catastrophic selection of the very worst tunes of 1678.

'Sorry. Can't be done,' said the saucy fellow. 'I would love to, I really would. But it's a logical thing. A world with Martin Smotheringale could not, by any reasonable definition that I am aware of, be considered to be the best of all possible worlds. *Reductio ad absurdum.*' Saying which, he unappeared, taking his menagerie with him.

Good God, what cheek! The ingratitude! And to the President of the Society no less. Left alone, I gazed morosely at the dung, urine and blood left by his parade of preposterous phantasmagoria. Sad to say, but there are times when I do hate quantum physics.

In honour of my service I was awarded the Order of Quantum Entanglement. This is not an award to be worn lightly, as it has the unfortunate tendency to entangle itself in all it passes. Its entanglement in the hoof of the Great One-Legged One was particularly notable. He was not pleased. The quantum is not something to be tangled with lightly.

The Curious Case of the Quantum Kittens

I had nearly finished dusting the Great One-Legged One on a day which we at the Society now refer to officially as *That Extraordinary Day*. I'd escaped the dusting with a mild goring of the liver, nothing too serious, and a rather flatter toe than I was used to on my left foot. He was still a feisty fellow, despite his millennia. Dear God, thank goodness we only dusted once a century or so.

I decided to send my assistant, Dr Dudley Morkleberry, a callow youth of some ninety winters, in to dust the Hypercube, while I attended, with some small annoyance, to the Perpetual Irritation Machine. The more I cleaned the blessed thing, the messier it got. Entropy is particularly annoying, as it was no doubt aware. I wonder sometimes why we keep it.

Morkleberry had come to us at the tender age of fifty, a recent graduate of the highly prestigious School for Scandal. Having graduated at only his thirteenth attempt, he was clearly a lad with promise and we had hastened to employ him. Out of the side of my left monocle, I saw him enter the Cube in what was, perhaps, an overconfident manner. Still, stout fellow! The Hypercube was no place for the fainthearted. Or anyone, when one gave it thought. All this was admirable, though unremarkable. It was his exit some three minutes later that roused my interest. Stout was not the term you would apply to what emerged. When I say emerged, good manners and decency would assume an emergence in the one place at the one time. Not on this day. The good Morkleberry had taken the liberty of emerging from four exits simultaneously. A quarter of Morkleberry each. He had looked quite drawn recently, but to be quartered strained belief. Dear God, why do we leave these tasks to the young? And the Cube was not even clean.

'Get back in the Hypercube and pull yourself together, Morkleberry!'

'Easy for you to say.' His voice resonated from more than the usual number of dimensions.

Despite his impertinence, all of him re-entered and re-emerged, this time from a single exit. He was all in one piece, but with his ears on backwards. I assured him that he could go back in, turn four and a half degrees into the fourth dimension and sort it out. He assured me that he would rather eat his left leg (which used to be his right, as it now turned out) than re-enter the Cube in this, or any subsequent, lifetime.

As he did not appear to be imminently inclined to consume the said appendage, I left him for my duties at the quantum Catbox. The Schrödinger bequest. The most famous catcoffin in quantum history. On the lid, written in blood, was the fearsome warning:

EXTREME DANGER!

NEVER TO BE OPENED

NOT IN THIS UNIVERSE

(Erwin Schrödinger, 1935)

This warning was taken seriously by the Society. I well remember the day in 1936 that an ashen-faced Dr Schrödinger delivered the beast/non-beast in a box to Sir Snedley. He was a tall, nervous man with ivory hair, this being well before ivory products were banned. 'Sir Snedley, after endless irritation from this scion of Satan, in the name of science and sanity I placed this appalling animal in a suppositional state. I threw in the oldest lump of uranium I could find, my third worst Geiger counter and a vial of poison gas. If the uranium decays, the Geiger counter clicks, and the very expensive poison gas kills the benighted beast. Until some fool looks in the Catbox to see what happened, he is both living and dead. Oh, and I threw in a very comfy cushion. I am not a monster!'

Sir Snedley assured him that this had been farthest from his mind which, as it happened, it was. Many things were.

'I had to do it. It wasn't only the science. It was an appalling animal living. It would be an even more appalling animal dead. Yet, Sir Snedley, imagine it being both at once, as it is now, and if it were to get out of the Catbox without anyone looking? Not alive, not dead. It could appear everywhere, anywhen. I cannot accept such responsibility. I trust only the Society to guard this catastrophe. As a precaution, I have written a warning in blood on the lid. Never let it out, Sir Snedley, and never look in the Catbox. I formally entrust it, in perpetuity, to the care of the Society.'

These words rang in my ears as I approached the Catbox. I froze in horror. The ringing came not from those words, nor even my rather alarming tinnitus. It was the Catbox escape alarm. I ran to the Catbox. Dear God, it was open! No cat, no corpse. An awful, unresolved feline absence. The benighted beast had escaped, unobserved. As no one had looked in the Catbox to see what had happened, off it had happily gone, living and dead. The consequences for this universe were unimaginable. Others more so, perhaps. A living dead cat was free to roam the cosmos, terrifying all with its superpositional insouciance. God forfend, if it were to enter the Hypercube it might breed with alternate versions of itself, ad infinitum. A countless clowder of quantum cats, flicking in and out of existence everywhere at once, caterwauling through every nook of the universe. This could certainly cause difficulties for the Society. We might even have to move universes, absorbing all the sundry costs involved.

To uphold the honour of the Society, solemn holders of the Cat, and to save reality from itself, I had to get them both back in the Catbox. Dead and alive.

Where was the infernal animal? Enlisting his new-found reverse auditory powers, I asked Morkleberry to close his eyes and face the front door, so that he could hear if they came in the back. Suddenly there was a cacophony of barking, coming from our famous canine collection. Pavlov's Dogs had heard the alarm, and sensed what they took to be lunch. I ran into the collection room. Good God, there was a lake of saliva coming from these conditioned canines. Litres of the stuff were slopping round the floor. Most unsnairy!

I recalled that a nervous-looking Dr Pavlov had dropped them off. 'Please, under no circumstances ring any alarms while I am away. The consequences could be atrocious.' He assured me that he would be right back to pick them up, and ran out the door. That was back in 1890. I was starting to wonder if he had been delayed. The pack was sailing across the sea of saliva, on the tail of the errant feline.

I half-glimpsed the beast as it ran, wailing all the while, from the pack. The living parts were flailing wildly, after their long captivity and with a pack of psychotic pooches on the hunt. The dead were much more laidback, but clearly happy to be liberated. Confronted by a rising tide of saliva, and the cacophony of conditioned canines, the beast ran straight for the nearest refuge. The Hypercube. Dear God, it was in the Cube. I held my breath, in a small bag I kept on hand for such occasions, and waited. I did not have to wait long.

It was as I feared. Out they pawed from every exit, yowling in their legions. One rather handsome family group had their heads on back to front, while another group of post-modernists wore all their internal organs on the outside. Yet another group, in what was clearly a great evolutionary advance, had legs on their backs so they could rest while walking. All, however, were dead/alive. It was a most disturbing, and noisy, spectacle.

How to get this lot back in the Catbox? One had been daunting enough. And now the Dogs were closing in, still riding the tide of saliva. The wave would hit us all soon.

'Dear God, turn the alarm off, Morkleberry, before we all drown,' I cried. Unfortunately, being at the front door with his ears the wrong way round, he did not hear this desperate plea. The tide continued to rise.

The Clowder, formerly known as Cat, had only two options. Either they all got in the Catbox, or they all ran out the door past Dr Morkleberry, who was standing there with his eyes wide shut, as directed, straining hard to hear backwards. While this sight perplexed them, it was an option. After a period of sustained and purposeful dithering, I realised I was getting nowhere. What to do?

It was, however, through no deed of Morkleberry or myself that the stand-off was resolved. It was the Great One who intervened. And intervene he did. He was not fond of cats. An infinite number of living/dead quantum cats was not at all to his liking. This was too much, even for one who lived in close proximity to the Perpetual Irritation Machine. With a mighty thump of his Great Leg he collapsed the wave function, and a goodly part of the floor. Probability be damned. And so it was. Or at least chastened.

All was quiet. Dead and alive, they had, as one, felt that the Catbox was a far better place to be than under the Great Leg. Blindfolding myself, I quickly lifted the lid and threw in a new lump of old uranium, a new Geiger counter and a fresh vial of expensive poison gas. Given the new arrivals, in an act of rash generosity, I threw in an extra comfy cushion. I slammed down the lid and locked the Catbox. I waited. I rather fancied that I could hear a large number of cats calling from somewhere in the ether. Or not. All was back to normal.

I put a large lock on the Catbox, reset the alarm, fed the Dogs and mopped the floor. Pouring myself, Morkleberry and the Great One a stiff Liversludge Gin, I reflected on the day's events. I do hate Dusting Day.

While I was pouring the Liversludges Morkleberry was, as tradition dictates, preparing a rather lavish awards ceremony. I was honoured to receive the Star of Feline Felicity with Oak Cluster. The cluster was rather heavy, being seventeen kilograms of real oak in honour of the gravity of the award. After three days spent lying face down on the floor, I eventually summoned the strength of chest and will to parade proudly with my award through our office to great acclaim from all.

The Ghosts of Gridley Gorge

I would be distressed beyond measure if readers of these tales should form the view that the Society's work is confined to our office at Great Snarkley Street, although a great many extraordinary events do occur there. We are by no means a deskbound Society.

I was busy one morning inspecting Morkleberry's skull for cracks (the lad had complained that ideas seemed to leak from his head) when I received a call from Lady Bloglingdon-Snype of Gridley Gorge Manor concerning what she described as a 'particularly nasty haunting'. I had left young Morkleberry to mind the office, to attend to the matter myself. This was no job for a lad not yet one hundred, and with no social standing. No, this particular inquiry required experience and eminence. This was a job for the

Society President, and none other. I had the greatest confidence that I would solve this absurd mystery. My confidence was well placed, as the reader will discover.

Gridley Gorge Manor is a stately pile, built in 1357, adjacent to the eponymous gorge. Local legend has it that Gridley Gorge is infinitely deep. Sadly, this was not the case, as I was to discover at a later date when we attempted to hide the infinitely long Gap inside it. Infinite indeed! It was a good five metres short.

The drive from our office to the Manor gates takes an hour or so, with a further three hours up the Manor driveway. I whiled away the journey counting backwards from infinity, a trick I find always fills in some time.

The door was opened by the butler, Blithers, whom I knew had butlered many colourful identities, including Vlad the Impaler, Attila the Hun and Caligula. Such dedication to service was rare these days. I was not surprised to find him in such august surrounds. I was shown to the library, where Lady Bloglingdon-Snype was busy oppressing the proletariat. Whilst she was thus occupied, I screwed in my monocles and took the opportunity to examine my host. She was an imperious and impressive person, though unusual in some respects. She was taller than she was wide, for a start, but then so many are these days. Interestingly, she had legs so long that they both touched the ground *at the same time*. A remarkable woman indeed.

Sending the proletariat on his way, duly chastened, she turned to greet me. She was clearly shaken, and somewhat stirred.

'Dr Smotheringale, thank you for coming. This is a most unpleasant and terrifying business, and I am at my wit's end. I have tried various spiritualists, but to no avail. They simply fill the room with incense and nonsense.' Her hands being damp with anxiety, and not having a clothesline handy, she held them out to drip dry. Ah, the aristocracy! Such elegance.

'I need a man of *science*, such as yourself. Dr Smotheringale, after a hiatus of more than three hundred years, the Ghosts of Gridley Gorge have returned.'

Dear God, I thought, not those horrendous horrors. Even an experienced absurdist such as I had trepidations in dealing with these portentous phantasms. And I speak as one who has dealt with half-dead cats and worse.

The Lady continued. 'Death always follows their appearance, and such was the case last week. I implore the Society to look into this matter. It is an unusual, alarming and possibly absurd kind of haunting.'

'Lady Bloglingdon-Snype, the resources of the Society are at your service. Now, given the gravity of the situation, I will break the habit of a lifetime, and ask you to start at the very beginning. Not a very good place to start, but a place nonetheless.'

Through quivering lips (which were not her own, as it so happened), she told me of the following extraordinary ectoplasmic events. The apparitions had appeared on three occasions, each resulting in the sudden death of a family member. In each visitation, three undead intruders were seen. The first appearance occurred in 1388, shortly after the Manor was constructed. There was a great feast being held in the Dining Hall. Suddenly, three apparitions appeared out of the wall, red of face and each armed with a knife, running in single file across the Hall. They appeared to be in furious pursuit of some unknown aim. Each waved a fearsome knife at the assembled company as they ran, then all leapt into the fireplace and disappeared. Duke Ogbert de Snype, a man of timorous disposition and poor health, fell down stone dead in shock. An exorcism was held, and the murderous apparitions were not heard of for over three hundred years.

The next appearance of the three ghastly Ghosts occurred in 1705. Duke Marmenduke de Snype had recently returned from the Continental Wars, and was celebrating with friends in the Grand Ballroom. Now, the Duke was a rotund, rubicund *bon vivant*. His stout heart was well able to deal with the rigours of battle. And yet it was, I fear, no match for the Ghosts. In the middle of the ballroom they appeared, again waving knives and in furious pursuit of some ephemeral excess. In single file they leapt into the wall and disappeared. As with his ancestor, the Duke fell down, stone dead.

Since then, nothing had been seen or heard of this terrible triumvirate until last week. Lady Hoglington, a cousin of my host, was having a cheeky morning Liversludge Gin in the Great Kitchen with Baron Dumbleton. The hogsheads had just been filled ('We use real hogs' heads, Dr Smotheringale. An advantage of living in the country.') when the ghastly trio burst forth from the pantry and waved knives in her general direction, before disappearing into the oven. The good Lady Hoglington fell back in shock, tumbling out the window to her death amongst Lady Bloglingdon-Snype's rhododendrons.

'As you can see, Dr Smotheringale, we live in terror of the return of the trio of terror.'

'Fear not, Lady Bloglingdon-Snype, I have no doubt we can solve this frightful mystery, and banish these defenestrating demons from the Manor.'

So saying, I began to poke around the various rooms in question. This did not evoke the feel of the undead. No, this smacked of human malevolence. *Hello.* Just as I suspected: Wormholes. Good Lord! The place was absolutely riddled with them.

I have frequently been asked how one can distinguish a Wormhole, a link through time and space, from a simple wormhole, one actually made by a worm. This is no easy task. Indeed, the only way to accurately gauge the status of a hole is to enter it. On numerous occasions I have entered a wormhole, confidently expecting to appear in Alpha Centauri, or some such place, only to find myself face to face with a very large, and angry, worm. It is only then one knows that one has entered a lower-case wormhole. And that the worm may not only be angry, but hungry. Caution is always advised.

'Lady Bloglingdon-Snype, I do not believe that your hauntings are due to the deceased. It is far worse than that. As I suspected, my Lady, the Manor is full of Wormholes.'

'Sir, you forget yourself!' she cried indignantly.

'Temporal-spatial Wormholes, Lady Bloglingdon-Snype. Links between different times and places. You walk in and walk out somewhere and somewhen else. They are quite expensive to buy, you know.' Such talk of status had the effect of calming her considerably. 'My good Lady, I vow by the honour of the Society to catch these miscreants, and end the reign of terror of the Ghosts of Gridley Gorge.'

I took out my bronze dirk. It was a gift from Sir Snedley, which he used during the Trojan War. An arrow killed Achilles? Nonsense. It was Sir Snedley and his dirk. If it worked for a demigod, it would do for a Ghost. This looked like a grim business, and I was prepared for the worst. Three armed, rough rapscallions who would haunt a family through time and space, killing successive generations though sheer terror, like the Great One-Legged One, were not to be trifled with lightly. There was nothing else for it, I would have to retrace the steps of the fiends, and put an end to these appalling apparitions.

I decided to find the largest Wormhole and leap in, leaving an astonished Lady Bloglingdon-Snype in my wake and the 21st century. Excellent so far, I thought. No worms. This was definitely an Upper Caser. I had leapt forth into what appeared to be a mediaeval banquet. Aha, the right place and time. Late 14th century. I could see a well-dressed, regal fellow of sallow disposition, whom I assumed to be the Duke. He looked decidedly ill, and rather wobbly on his feet. He was clearly immensely disturbed, so the Ghosts must have been here recently. I waved my dirk in his general direction so as to assure him that I was on his side. No sign of them. They must be ahead. I had the curious feeling I was being followed. Still, no time to turn around now. I leapt into the hall's fireplace, the most likely way they had gone, according to legend.

Thank God, another Upper Caser. My face was burning with exertion, righteous anger, and a slight singeing from the fire. I emerged in the middle of what looked like a ballroom. Early 18th century. Excellent. A rather rotund, rubicund fellow, whom from the Lady's description I took to be the Duke, looked mortally ill. So the apparitions had already been through here also. Still no sign of them. I waved my dirk at him to indicate my support, and jumped into the nearest wall. Yet another Upper Caser. I still had the odd feeling of being followed, but I was hot on their heels, so no time for inspection.

There I was, in a kitchen, with an aristocratic-looking woman and man sipping from hogsheads. The remainders of the hogs lay nearby. Lady Hoglington appeared rather wobbly on her feet and, I feared, far too near the window. Waving my dirk in benediction at her, I jumped into the oven, where our miscreants had been seen to head, and appeared in the library, from whence I started. Lady Bloglingdon-Snype appeared rather surprised to see me. Odd. A perfectly quotidian materialisation. Still, no time for niceties. I still had not caught up with them. Only one thing for it. I had to retrace my steps and hope to get there earlier to catch these knife-wielding maniacs.

I immediately started my journey again. Leaping back into the 14th century, I saw my quarry. At least one of them. Where were the rest? I waved my dirk at the distressed Duke in solidarity, and leapt after the spirit. I still had the uncanny feeling there was someone behind me. I leapt into the 18th century after my foe, hot on his tail. This Duke appeared apoplectic, even after I waved my dirk in support. Back in the

21st century kitchen, waving my dirk in abandoned pursuit, I rushed past Lady Hoglington, who still appeared *far* too near the window, jumped into the oven and out into the Library. No sign of them there either. Again, I repeated my pursuit of these ghastly apparitions through the centuries. Hello, now there were two of them. We were making progress, and I no longer felt I was being followed. So where was the third? Bounding through the Wormholes, I doggedly persisted. I lost sight of them, and landed in the library in the present (at least, as present as possible in such circumstances), in front of the not-inconsiderable bulk of Lady Bloglingdon-Snype.

'Dr Smotheringale, will you *please* stop disappearing into the wall. It is unnerving and unseemly.'

'My apologies, my Lady. Please allow me a moment to think.'

'We do not, sir, approve of such fripperies in the Manor.'

'My sincere apologies, my Lady, but I fear it is necessary in this case.'

I was, of course, sympathetic to her view. As readers of these tales will be aware, thought is my option of last resort. I am a believer in action, but on the odd occasion I have found thinking to be of some marginal use. Now, let me see what we knew. Three knife-wielding maniacs. Now, how many times had I looped through? Three, at last count. Did I have my old dirk on each occasion? Yes. Red-faced? Well, I was glowing from the exertion of the chase. And then there was that feeling of being followed that had so curiously ceased on the third run through. Mmmm.

I leapt up in a moment of ecstatic enlightenment. Yes! That was it. The mystery was solved! What a triumph for the Society. The resolution of one of the greatest mysteries of the ages. Your humble scribe is far too modest to mention the personal acclaim that could come from this extraordinary investigation.

'Lady Bloglingdon-Snype, I can categorically assure you that the Ghosts of Gridley Gorge will not infest the Manor again.'

'This is wonderful news, Dr Smotheringale. Have you caught the miscreants?'

'My Lady, I have done far better than that. I *am* the miscreants!'

I informed her, triumphantly, that the three knife-wielding apparitions were, in point of fact, me chasing myself through time and space, waving a friendly dirk in the direction of the various family members. What they took to be the Ghosts were merely my good self vigorously carrying out the investigation into the Ghosts of Gridley Gorge. 'Three of me, in hot pursuit of myself.'

The Lady appeared deeply impressed by my revelation. Or at least she turned very pale and sat down, which amounts to the same thing. The relief of knowing her torment was at an end, I surmised sagely.

'Sir, are you saying that it was *your very investigation* that killed my relatives?'

'Indeed, my Lady, I can confidently say that it was. It is, as you can clearly see, a triumph for the Society's investigative techniques. For without this thorough investigation, I fear that the matter would never have been resolved.'

The good Lady made a statement to the effect that, without my intervention, her relatives might have lived long and noble lives, and her rhododendrons would be in far better condition. Pure sophistry, I privately reflected, although I was far too polite to say this. She was distressed, and clearly not thinking straight. Ghosts will do that to you.

In triumph, I retired from the Manor. It is such selfless devotion to duty that lies at the very heart of the Society, as I later declaimed to an impressed Morkleberry, as we held a solemn ceremony awarding me the Society's Cross of Valour for Psychical Research.

The Search for the Missing Gap

I do not blame young Morkleberry for the manner in which events unfolded. I could, of course, if I felt so moved, but I blame myself. 'No, no, Dr Smotheringale!' I hear you cry. I thank you warmly for your trust and support.

Now, for the first time, I will disclose the events of that fateful day. The reader is well advised to place no credence on the sensationalist headlines that gained prominence in the press ('*Universe to end at 4pm last Tuesday*', '*Everywhere and everywhen is here now*'). It is you, loyal and valued peruser of these tales, who will be the first outside the hallowed halls of 13 Great Snarkley Street to hear the truth. I fear I must advise those of a timid disposition, or who are easily shocked, to read no further for the sake of their health and sanity. We at the Society value life, as our remarkable intervention at Gridley Gorge amply demonstrated, and do not wish to provoke any unnecessary cardiovascular crises. To those made of sterner stuff, I entreat you to pour yourself a stiff Liversludge, put on an extra pair of socks and brace yourself.

It all started innocently enough. We had been in desperate need for some time of a pig in a poke to keep Schrödinger's Clowder company. I had sent Morkleberry out to market, with the Society's chequebook, to buy said porker. I would not, under normal circumstances, have entrusted him so, but had accidentally got my head stuck in the Insanitiser that morning, whilst cleaning out some old ideas. I had to keep an eye on that. Insanity, like inanity, is highly addictive. In any case it was the first time he had been so entrusted, and he was clearly excited, jumping from foot to foot like the stripling nonagenarian he is.

It was only when Morkleberry returned to Great Snarkley Street that I became aware that things had *not* gone to plan. He had no poke. He had no pig. What he did have surprised even your scribe and, as it so happened, the denizens of a number of nearby universes.

According to Morkleberry, it happened as follows. He had left the premises, a spritely skip in his step and chequebook in hand, looking forward to completing his first commission. I smiled wistfully, recalling nostalgically the carefree days of my first century. He was nearing the market when he espied a rather suspicious fellow, standing idly in a trench, wearing a *particularly* large trench coat. But then, as the observant Morkleberry noted, it was a *particularly* large trench. I approved strongly of this sartorial detail. Always dress to suit the occasion, I say.

As Morkleberry passed, the fellow addressed him. 'Hello there, young lad, wither away?' The accent, according to Morkleberry, was strongly suggestive of Proxima Centauri. This should have warned the lad. No good has ever come from there.

'I am going to buy a pig in a poke on behalf of the Society for the Preservation of Preposterous Absurdity. I have the Society chequebook,' he helpfully informed the gentleman.

'Ah, the Society. Excellent. Well, you don't want no pig in a poke, son. What you want is a Gap. Not any old Gap either. This one here is a long Gap. A very long Gap indeed. In fact, laddie, it is infinitely long! Just the thing for the front office. Just think how pleased your boss will be with a Gap.'

Now, if Morkleberry had been perhaps only some eighty or so years older, he may have been more wary of purchasing a Gap, rather than a pig. One cannot, however, put an old head on young shoulders, as the Society found out surgically late last century.

'Do you really think so?' the naive young fellow asked.

'Certainly, young man.'

'May I ask, what is a gap?'

'Certainly, young fellow,' he vouchsafed.

'What is a gap, sir?'

'Not a gap. A Gap.'

'A Gap?'

'The most Absent Absence you've ever seen. There is nothing emptier than this Gap. Just think, no other Society in the cosmos would have such a distinct Lack of Everything.'

Well, imagine the circumstance. Young Morkleberry, anxious to please, with brass in pocket and an infinitely long Gap before him. The lad did not think twice. As I said, I blame myself. I should have procured the porker myself. The temptation was too great for Morkleberry and, of course, gold and Gap soon changed hands.

'Did you at least measure the object before you purchased it?'

'Indeed, Dr Smotheringale. I am not a complete fool. Merely an incomplete one. It took some time, but it is indeed, as the man said, infinitely long.'

'Hmm. And how much did he want for an infinitely long Gap?'

'A gold bar per metre, Dr Smotheringale.'

'A gold bar per metre?' I bellowed. 'Outrageous! I trust you haggled?'

'Indeed, sir. I drove a hard bargain. I beat him down to *half* a gold bar per metre.'

'Well done, young fellow.' Half an infinite number of gold bars did seem a bargain. I would have preferred the pig in a poke, but there was no help for it now. You should never look a gift horse in the mouth, they say. If only they had ignored this adage at Troy, back in the day, things might have turned out rather differently. We would have to make do and, I feared, remain pigless. 'What is the provenance of the object? From whence did it come?'

'The man said that it had fallen off the back of an infinitely long truck.'

Hmm. Well, there was no choice now. Here it was, on our very doorstep, and we had to accommodate it. It was up to us to mind the Gap. I screwed in both monocles to get a better look at the Absence.

'All right. Let's get it into the vestibule. Morkle-berry, you grab one end, or lack thereof, and I'll take the other.' Getting to our respective ends took some time, as it so transpired. Indeed, far longer than I thought possible. In any case, I was footsore and weary upon reaching the end.

It was then that our troubles commenced. We hefted the Gap upon our shoulders, and entered the office. I was certain that if we got the angles right, it would fit in nicely beside the Perpetual Irritation Machine. That was the theory. Praxis proved to be somewhat more difficult.

The first thing I heard was the window at the end of the hall breaking. I looked up to see an Absence in the middle of the pane, and the Gap poking through into the street. 'Dear God, Morkleberry, be careful.'

We were backing up when the telephone rang. It was a chap calling from some thirty kilometres away, complaining of being poked in the eye by a ridiculously long Gap. I apologised, and sought other solutions. We had paid good money for this, and I was determined to add it to our treasures. Sideways wasn't working. Let's try for up, I reasoned. Up we hefted it, on its end, or at least as much of an end as we had the time to locate. More noise – this time a flurry of plaster and tiles disappearing into the Absence. It had poked a hole through the roof, kept on going, and poked a hole through Mars, and goodness knows what else.

This was no good. We had to get it outside, somewhere big enough to hold the blessed thing. Of course! Gridley Gorge. It was rumoured to be infinitely deep by a great number of possibly intoxicated locals. Just the ticket. We could store it there and charge admission. Lady Bloglingdon-Snype, I had no doubt, would be pleased to host the Gap, after our triumph in banishing the Ghosts of Gridley Gorge. Indeed, once we assured her that there were no Ghosts or Upper Casers involved, nor any of her late relatives, she was pleased to assist.

'Are you sure the Gorge will be deep enough, Dr Smotheringale?' she enquired.

'Infinitely certain, my Lady,' I assured the worthy woman.

So, off we went afoot, balancing the Gap end-up between us. As readers will be aware, it is a fair walk to Gridley Gorge from our office, and we made quite a sight as we attempted to avoid poking holes through passing aircraft. Still, there are costs to be paid for any great advance. With huge relief, we came to Gridley Gorge and started to drop the Gap into the Gorge. Excellent, I thought, as it continued to unappear, so to speak. And then, we hit the bottom. With some of the Gap *still* poking out. *Quite* a lot in fact. The so-called infinite Gorge had a bottom. Who would have thought it? Not Morkleberry nor I, as we are trusting souls. No good: we had to get it back to Great Snarkley Street and try again. So, off we went, balancing the preposterous Gap between us.

We had just arrived back at the office, when it hit me. Why, I do not know, but it did. In any case, recovering, I had an inspiration. The Hypercube! Of course, we could pop it in there. Slip it in through the fourth dimension.

'Morkleberry, we'll pop it in the Hypercube. Gently lower it, and hold onto the middle. I'll be hanged if I am going to walk to the end again.'

'Where exactly is the middle of an infinitely long Gap, Dr Smotheringale?'

The impertinence of the young! I gave it some thought. Here was as good as anywhere, I reasoned, and far less time to travel. 'Just about anywhere, young lad, just about anywhere,' I uttered avuncularly. 'Here will do just fine.'

So saying, we hefted the thing and gradually pushed it into the Cube. It was then that tragedy struck. We were just finishing getting the blessed thing in, when it slipped from our hands. Morkleberry, with his reverse ears, had failed to hear my instructions properly, as I had spoken them, like the gentleman I am, to his front. Damn those ears! It must be said that, despite a voice described in several aural fashion magazines as 'mellifluous and a thing of beauty', I have a tendency to mumble on occasion. This comes from my firm conviction that wisdom must not be too widely bestowed, and from a desire to conserve the world's oxygen. Yes, reader, I can hear you thinking *noblesse oblige*. You are too kind. We in the Society live to serve.

It was at this very instance that reality started to fray. Holes started appearing in time and space. Large holes through which the preposterous was happily parading itself. Next week's lunch was being served two weeks ago in the boardroom. A meeting that concluded in May 1543 was about to commence in the library. Meanwhile, Sir Snedley, far less dead than he used to be, was a picture of dignity, quietly going about his business as if nothing had happened. Which it had. Meanwhile, whatever that term meant in these circumstances, the room was filling up rapidly with a seemingly infinite number of alternate Smotheringales and Morkleberries, gesticulating wildly at us. One alternate Smotheringale was wearing a *single* monocle. Extraordinary! It was beginning to get very crowded as yet more alternates appeared, each speaking urgently of a missing Gap.

What could this all mean? It was only then that I finally realised what we had on our hands. Dear God, this was not any old gap. Or, indeed, any old Gap. This was *the* Gap between universes. The Gap was missing. And we had lost it. This could get very unsnairy indeed. Everything and everywhen was coming here and now.

Someone would have to enter the Hypercube, and search for the missing Gap. Speaking from behind so he could hear me, I bellowed through the gathering din, 'Morkleberry! I fear you must enter the Cube, and retrieve the missing Gap. The multiverse depends upon it.'

Morkleberry reminded me of his solemn oath never to enter the Cube again in this, or any possible future, existence. I pointed out to the lad that he might well get his ears back on frontwards, and have his left leg back on the left. He informed me that he rather liked them the way they were. I must say that I could see his point. Quite the ladies' man these days, was young Morkleberry, with his fashionable reverse ears. And with reverse legs, he was a terror on the dance floor. He was also having a rather fine time chatting with a largish crowd of various alternate Morkleberries. Such is youth. There was nothing else for it. I, Smotheringale, would have to retrieve the Gap. I entered the Cube. *Noblesse oblige* indeed!

A tricky business, finding a missing Gap. Where to look? Nowhere that there was something would be the most obvious place to start. Looking around, there were things everywhere. I decided upon action. I rushed off at full throttle in one direction, only to appear backwards, facing upwards. I repeated the manoeuvre some fifteen times, to the same effect. All this running had gotten me exactly nowhere, I reflected. Then it hit me. *Nowhere* was exactly where I was. Just the place for a Gap to hide. And there it was! Hiding its Absence in the Absence. I allowed myself some small satisfaction. What excellent management upon my part!

Now to get out with the Gap. Running wasn't going to get me anywhere. There was nothing for it. I removed my monocles, closed my eyes and leapt backwards in a reverse quadruple pike and turn, and landed Somewhere. Good enough. I dived out the nearest exit, carrying the Gap exultantly upon my shoulder. As the Gap emerged from the Cube, the various alternative Smotheringales and Morkleberries, who had got on remarkably well, cheered and said their farewells, as our realities parted company for the foreseeable past.

Despite this triumph, I was somewhat despondent. After all this, we *still* had to find a place to put the Gap. Hmm. 'How long was that particularly large trench, Morkleberry?'

'Very long indeed, Dr Smotheringale. I could not see the end.'

'You have excellent eyesight, I believe?'

'Indeed, sir.'

'No end at all?'

'No, sir, not in either direction.'

'Good enough.'

So, at midnight, we took the Gap back to the trench from whence it came, and under cover of dark quietly dropped it in. There was no sign of the cad who had sold the thing to Morkleberry, or our half an infinite number of gold bars. We carefully covered it up as best we could, and there it resides to this day, quietly doing its work.

Upon reflection, I believe that it may fairly be said that the events of the day were yet another magnificent success for the Society, born though it was from Morkleberry's youthful ignorance.

'Young Morkleberry,' I opined, my eyes moistening with pride, 'never forget that upon this day reality and the multiverse were saved. And solely through our efforts! Without us, there would be chaos!' Unfortunately, I was facing Morkleberry's front, so he did not hear me.

Upon our return to Great Snarkley Street, we held a small ceremony in which I was presented with the Award for Multiversal Excellence. I made a brief three-hour speech, entitled '*We live to serve*', which was well received by Morkleberry and, indeed, the Great One-Legged One, who attended in formal attire. I still rather wished, though, that we had a pig.

A Matter of the Utmost Gravity

All was peaceful. The Perpetual Irritation Machine was in low gear, Schrödinger's Clowder were half-dead on their feet, and the Great One-Legged One was munching contentedly on leftover pieces of reality. The reader will be aware that such repose is rare, as events frequently require our active intervention to save life, limb and, on occasion, the multiverse. Preposterity, like rust and the Great One-Legged One, never sleeps. I had taken this break in events to work on my latest necrography, *Great Corpses of the 20*th *Century*. I admit shyly to the reader that I had great hopes for the work as a Hollywood screenplay. The funds from such an enterprise would have been most welcome, as we were still paying out the half an infinite number of gold bars for the Gap. We would be on solid financial ground again only when we had acquitted the debt. I was thus engaged when young Morkleberry came gambolling into the room bearing sobering news, and waving a copy of *The Torpid Times*. A remarkable paper, *The Times*, boasting as it did that it printed all, and only, the news not fit to print.

'Dr Smotheringale! Dr Smotheringale! They have found the gravity waves!'

'What! Good heavens!' I blanched, visibly, at this distressing news. I do not know why, but at any distressing news I feel an irrepressible urge to retire to the Society kitchen and blanch. Always visibly, of course.

'And we hid them so well,' I asserted morosely from the kitchen, saucepan in hand.

I cast my mind back to the day that we accidentally created the accursed things. Given the responsibilities we at the Society nobly bear, we find ourselves in occasional need of some harmless recreation. It was in this spirit that I had decided to install an artificial beach in the attic. I had imported several hundred thousand tonnes of sand, and a goodly proportion of the Pacific Ocean, using the Wandering Wormhole, an Upper Caser of no fixed abode that we had procured from Gridley Gorge Manor, much to the relief of Lady Bloglingdon-Snype. After our adventures with the Ghosts, she appeared to have developed a rather inexplicable aversion to Upper Casers.

Fortunately, the attic is a rather large room, as I strive always for authenticity. I had even installed a killer whale to endow the place with a homely feel. What we needed, though, were waves. Morkleberry, like so many men in their nineties, was a keen bodysurfer. Getting the bodies was the most difficult part. We at the Society, however, have great influence in all strata of society, even amongst the recently deceased. We enquired at the Cemetery for the Chronically Dead and, like the good souls they were, they viewed *any* service to the Society a singular honour.

Accordingly, I had ordered a wave machine through the post from a firm called Einstein Enterprises. They were a reputable mail-order firm, although they specialised mostly in faster-than-light particles, and other such trinkets. On the day in question, the package arrived. Morkleberry was beside himself as we unpacked the machine, which I found singularly unnerving. A hangover from his ordeal in the Hypercube, I presumed. The wave machine was inviting, bright and shiny, with Wave Maker Series 'G' stamped boldly on its lid. *Odd.* I could have sworn that I had ordered a Series W, with paddles. It also came with a somewhat peculiar warning for a wave machine.

> # USE WITH EXTREME CAUTION
>
> ## MAY CAUSE SUDDEN UNEXPECTED WEIGHT GAIN OR LOSS
>
> ## IF SYMPTOMS PERSIST, SEEK SOLACE

I could not see paddles or, indeed, any obvious means by which waves would be created. Still, I was no technician. We hauled it up to the attic and placed it on the shore of our beach. Morkleberry was in his swimmers, a fresh body tucked under his arm, jumping excitedly from foot to foot. There was a bright red on switch on top. Curiously, I could see no off switch. Still, once we had the surf up, we could let it run. I turned the device on, and heard a humming sound. Oh, dear God.

'Stop that Morkleberry! It's annoying.'

'Sorry, sir. I am excited.'

'Indeed. But where are the waves?'

Where indeed? We looked in disappointment at the calm sea, the only ripples coming from the killer whale, who was fixing us with an unnerving glare. I was beginning to think the beast might well be psychopathic. Perhaps we should not have purchased it from the high-security prison in Lower Snarkley Street, cheap though it was. They had seemed rather anxious to sell. In any case, we were standing in total bewilderment at what was not happening, only to be totally bewildered by what actually did.

It commenced with Morkleberry suddenly complaining that his body felt heavy, very heavy indeed, and that he could not hold it up anymore. I looked over to see his favourite corpse drop from his hands to the floor. Dear God, we were *all* dropping to the floor! It was worse than that. *Everything* was getting denser and being pulled together. The walls were closing in, and not as an existential metaphor. Morkleberry, with his bodyboard, was cheek by jowl with me, our heads firmly glued to the floor. The killer whale was alarmingly close, and looked even more dangerous now that it weighed several tonnes more. The Attic Ocean was desperately trying to invade the floor below, much to the annoyance of the Great One-Legged One. Mars, a planet I was particularly fond of, was *far* closer than I liked, although this preferred distance was, it must be said, a personal predilection. I do not claim to speak for others. What is happening, I wondered, as my brain was experiencing how it felt to be extremely dense indeed. For a moment, I thought that I was doomed to being compacted together with Morkleberry, his bodyboard and a killer whale that was trying to live up to its reputation.

And then, suddenly, it stopped. I had just had time enough to make this acute observation when off we went again, this time in reverse. Suddenly everything was flying apart, including your chronicler. On a positive note, the kilos were dropping at a rate that any dietician would have given their eyeteeth for. As it so happened, at a later date some dieticians did indeed send said eyeteeth through the post. We politely informed them that, while overwhelmed by their generosity, we had perfectly serviceable eyeteeth of our own. Morkleberry was busy dancing on the ceiling, to great effect I might add, while the killer whale was breaching the roof in defiance of all decency. I was admiring my svelte self as the ceiling headed towards a rapidly receding cosmos, when, blow me down (and the whale did exactly that), we were hurtling towards each other again. Good God! Morkleberry's left lung was doing its best to be at one with my liver, and an infinite amount of whale was enveloping us all.

Again, it stopped. I had another brief moment for thought. What could be causing this? The entire horrifying thing seemed to be coming in waves. Oh, God! Of course. I recalled the warning on the machine: *May Cause Sudden Unexpected Weight Gain Or Loss.* We had the *wrong* Wave Maker. A Series G, not a humble Series W with a paddle. The accursed thing was a *Gravity* Wave Maker. A reverse-cycle one, no less. And with *no* OFF switch. Damn that Einstein. How did he ever get a job in a patent office? This was most alarming. We would have no bodysurfing today, of that I was certain. And no solace, to boot. What to do? We could, of course, try and throw it in the Hypercube. But the Series G was so cumbersome that we might fall in ourselves, with reverse organs, and God only knows what else. No, that would not do at all. I was far too old for reverse legs. They were a young man's game. No, this abominable machine would have to be thrown somewhere a *long* way away. I pondered, all the while awaiting the next wave of rampant weight and sanity loss. Why not the Wandering Wormhole? If it could get the Attic Ocean in, it could get this woeful machine out. The thing was to get a hold of the Gravity Wave Maker, and get it into the Wormhole. We had to hope that the other end of the Wormhole was not currently two rooms away last week. Still, we had to chance it.

It took ten more waves before we managed to get the Gravity Wave Maker to the entrance of the Wormhole. Where, and when, was the other end of the Wormhole at this time?

'Morkleberry, quickly, what can you see at the other end?' I said, as our craniums collided in yet another wave.

'It looks very, very, very small, sir. Incredibly small. Very, very, very tiny indeed.'

'Hmm, I wonder if it will fit? What time is it at the other end?'

'Zero o'clock, sir.'

Zero o'clock? Odd, it was 13.7 billion o'clock here. Well, it would have to do. In the next lull we heaved the thing into the Wormhole, just as it was about to expand us all again. What happened next, I can't quite describe. I had never heard a bang like it. Indeed, I think that I may confidently assert that no one has heard a bigger bang than the one we caused. We hurriedly put the Wormhole away and waited to see what normality looked like. All was quiet. Still no waves for poor Morkleberry, but at least our weight was stable.

The entire experience dampened (if I may use such a pun) our enthusiasm for the beach. We drained the Attic Ocean back into the sea through the Wandering Wormhole. I read in *The Torpid Times* the next day some rather strident letters to the editor regarding sudden coastal flooding and a rise in sea levels of some ten metres. Dear God, were these the same citizens who complained when the sea receded ten metres after we *filled* the Attic? There was simply no pleasing some people. The several hundred thousand tonnes of sand we dumped in the Sahara resulted in a spate of learned, though misguided, research papers on the hidden mechanisms underlying encroaching desert sands. Hidden mechanisms, indeed! It was an Upper Caser. Honestly, what do they teach in science courses in these declining, latter days? Morkleberry gave up bodysurfing, and quietly returned the bodies to the Cemetery for the Chronically Dead. As for the killer whale, Morkleberry and I decided that this was a job for the Great One-Legged One. Sent forth, he made short work of the offending behemothic cetacean. We enjoyed excellent sushi for a long time thereafter.

I pulled my mind back from these awful events to what we choose to think of as the present, and the alarming news of the discovery of the waves. I did, at least, have a rather lovely collection of blanched almonds and whale brisket to soothe me. 'So where, exactly, did they find the waves, Morkleberry?' I enquired thoughtfully.

'At the very beginning of the universe, sir. They seem to think that they caused a rather large bang. A *very, very, very* Big Bang, indeed, so they say. Some say it caused the expansion of the universe, and all the misery that followed.'

'Indeed?' This clearly called for recognition and an awards ceremony! In this spirit, I was presented with the Society Medal for Excellence in Universal Expansion, and gave a particularly poignant speech entitled '*Of all things come good*' to Morkleberry, who was not listening, as he was facing me.

The Note Taker

I was sitting at the Society piano, playing a selection of polkas for the Great One-Legged One to dance to. His deft footwork was a sight that would bring tears to the eyes of the most hardened observer. I looked down on the keyboard, however, with considerable sadness: A–G, sharps and flats. Eight notes in a scale, indeed! How sad, how *confining*. I will admit to the reader that I was an accomplished pianist. 'Was?' I hear you rise up and cry. 'Surely a man of your extensive accomplishments, Dr Smotheringale, still is!' I am afraid, however, that the past tense is quite deliberate in this case. My expertise was formed back in the day when we had a note for *every* letter of the alphabet, and not the deplorable remnants that pass for scales in these latter days.

And we had rather more than just sharps and flats. Why, there were snarkleys (after which the street our office resides upon was named), flozbits and the ineffable ezriquom. If you, reader, had heard the beauty of a sonatina in Z snarkley major, or a concerto in Q flozbit minor, you would weep for the loss of all that was beautiful in music. It is said by some that Beethoven's deafness was induced solely by the monumental loss of the ezriquom. Indeed, he is believed to have stuck skewers through his ears rather than suffer the indignity of an eight-note scale. Apocryphal? Perhaps, but no better explanation has been forthcoming. In any case, his *Symphony in K Ezriquom Major* was a loss to the world.

It happened like this. As the reader would expect, in an august organisation such as the Society, we have a great many important and lengthy meetings. Indeed, on one famous occasion, Sir Snedley chaired a meeting which opened in 1543 to organise the celebration for the Centenary of the Society in 1553, a much-anticipated event. After innumerable speeches and points of order, however, the meeting finally closed in 1558, five years *after* the Centenary. Sir Snedley, as perspicacious as he was wise, was determined that we would not miss the Bicentenary, and immediately commenced the Planning meeting for the 1653 celebrations. Under his careful chairmanship, the meeting adjourned no less than three years *prior* to the event. This triumph of order and parliamentary proceedings resulted in Sir Snedley receiving the Society Medal for Meeting Brevity and Excellence. He wore it with pride and distinction.

One of the problems with meetings, and they are legion, is taking *accurate notes* of the discussions, deliberations and action points. I, to my shame, was not up to the task, a reflection of my youth at the time. Indeed, on one occasion I fell asleep through the entire second month of a three-month meeting, missing some three hundred resolutions and points of order. After this, we hired a fellow who offered to take minutes. Indeed, he did. As well as seconds, hours and whole days. A three-month meeting would be over in fifteen seconds, leaving temporal gaps in the lives of the worthy that were never to be retrieved. It transpired that the chap was trying to live forever by keeping time.

After the Great One-Legged One had dealt with the miscreant, I was asked by Sir Snedley to seek alternatives. I espied an advertisement in *The Torpid Times* from a Dr Notoriety, which read as follows.

HAVING TROUBLE WITH NOTES?

TRY THE ALL NEW, AMAZING, STEAM-DRIVEN

NOTE TAKER[©]

NOTES WILL NOT BOTHER YOU AGAIN!

Just the ticket, I enthused, in youthful ignorance. I left the Society office to seek this amazing technological advance. What a time to be alive! This being the early 1800s, I travelled via horseless carriage. The Society's funds did not run to equine transportation. Pulling it through town, I was given to wonder why we bothered with the blessed thing. Sir Snedley assured me, however, that horseless carriages were the way of the future. Foresight, as always!

I entered the establishment, and was met by Dr Notoriety himself. I was immediately impressed. A wooden eye, a glass jaw, and a pearl inlaid wrist. A man of the highest quality.

'So, young man, are you having trouble with notes?' he enquired.

'Yes, sir, a great deal of trouble.'

'Do you have a lot of notes to deal with?'

'Indeed, sir, a great many.'

'Well then, son, this is the machine for you,' he said, pointing to his invention, the Note Taker. I looked in admiration upon it. How to describe it? The only accurate description is that it resembled an inverted harpsichord. Impressive. Needless to say, money soon changed hands and I loaded the Note Taker onto the horseless carriage, and proceeded to pull it back to Great Snarkley Street. The device was set up in the Grand Meeting room in readiness for the next Society meeting.

It was at our annual Planning for Preposterity meeting that the troubles arose, troubles that were to change the course of musical history. We were, as is customary at the commencement of all Society meetings, singing the Society song: *Here to Help, Hope to Hinder*. I was proudly playing the piano forte, and Sir Snedley was holding forth in a rich baritone voice that he had purchased from a rich baritone. The chap was not using it anymore, due to chronic death. We had come to the nine-hundredth bar, where the melody line rose to an M flozbit, when ... *nothing*!

No M.

No flozbit.

Simply an amazing and appalling Absence. It was not that we had missed the note. There *was* no note. I looked quizzically at the score. The M ledger line was gone. Worse still, there was no M flozbit key on the keyboard. Odd. We were perplexed, but soldiered on to the next bar, with its particularly beautiful R-T-U triad when, again, *no* R, T or U. Absent. This was horrifying. Both the keyboard and the music score were getting *smaller*!

'Smotheringale, what on earth are you up to? Please cease it immediately!' Sir Snedley demanded.

'Indeed, sir, if only I knew what I was doing.'

I was profoundly puzzled. It was then that I espied a Z ezriquom flying through the air towards the Note Taker! People speak, metaphorically, of a note hanging in the air. What fools. We had the actuality. Indeed, they were not merely hanging, but *flying* through the air.

'It is the Note Taker, sir. It is acting eponymously!'

Indeed it was. It was taking notes at an alarming rate. Not just a key or score. It was taking their very *noteness*. If this continued, there would be no music left. Meanwhile, the Proceedings were *still* being left undone and unnoted! This was a catastrophe.

I could see the notes being sucked into the machine. X sharp, gone. Z snarkley, gone. And so on. We had lost everything up to K natural. Wasting no time on thought, I seized the Society mace. It was kept for ceremonial reasons, and for Sir Snedley to settle points of order. I smashed the apparatus! Over and over, did I smite it. Upon ceasing, I could hear vague echoes of lost notes, receding into nothingness. The Note Taker had taken its last note. It was beyond repair. Pitiful. All we had managed to save were notes A through G, and a few boring old flats and sharps. That's all. Snarkley, now a street name. The ezriquom, a distant legend. The flozbit! Gone, never to be heard again.

Sir Snedley and I immediately went around to the office of Dr Notoriety to seek answers for this outrage. After hearing our story, he assured us that he had built only the one Note Taker, and had no plans for any more.

'In my defence, Sir Snedley, Dr Smotheringale did say he wanted notes to be taken. And taken they were! Indeed, sir, I was true to my word. You did try turning on the reverse switch, did you not? It *was* mentioned in the instructions.' Needless to say, I had not wasted valuable Society time reading such nonsense as instructions.

'Instructions! Reverse switch, sir?' Sir Snedley thundered.

'Indeed, Sir Snedley, the notes would have come back. All of them. And even more notes would have been created! Beautiful notes and chords. Old and new. All lost to this reality. Forever. I suppose an eight-note scale *might* work,' he mused, 'but it is not much to work with.'

The Society immediately held an emergency meeting to discuss the events. The issues were complex. On the one hand, it was Dr Notoriety who had created the contraption. It was, however, your scribe, the Society's representative, who had turned it on. It was your scribe who neglected to notice, or use, the reverse button. It was your scribe who smashed the Note Taker beyond repair, losing almost all the notes in existence, for all time.

Sir Snedley, in his impeccable wisdom, decided there was only one honourable course of action. An awards ceremony, celebrating the Society's achievement in saving a modicum of music. I was presented with the Golden Star of Musical Preservation, which I wear proudly to this day. A great many famous musicians and composers of the day attended. It *was* a remarkable achievement, in retrospect. Beethoven was invited, but sent his apologies. Ear trouble, apparently.

The Negative Probability Generator

As with so many preposterous events, it started with a simple request, and what the Society believed was a simple solution. We had need of a generator. The amount of power required to run the Society's office was draining the national grid and, indeed, a great deal of the rest of the world's. Much of the planet was in perpetual blackout, which did little for our public relations.

The reasons for our high energy use were manifold. The Perpetual Irritation Machine, as its name suggested, ran constantly, and consumed a rather annoying amount of power. Keeping Schrödinger's Clowder simultaneously alive and dead was an energy-sapping business. They had to be kept warm and cool, to prevent illness and/or putrescence;

a tricky problem involving an inverse cycle air-conditioner that kept the Box simultaneously hot and frigid. The Hypercube sucked energy into an infinite number of dimensions, solely for its own pleasure, whilst the cost of running the Great One-Legged One's hoof warmer was astronomical. It *is* a large hoof, and one does not deny the Great One's comforts if one values living. Which we do. Such was the drain on power that the governments of the world, no less, had asked us to seek a solution. That they should turn to *us* for a solution clearly showed the high esteem in which the Society was held.

What to do? We could not, of course, close down any of our exhibits, all of which were of incalculable value. No, that would not do at all. Not wishing to exert myself with thought, my time being of paramount importance, I sought Morkleberry's opinion. He suggested that we simply purchase a generator.

'A capital idea!' I enthused. After all, what could go wrong? *Still*, given our experiences with the Gap and the Note Taker, for safety's sake, I thought it best if we *both* went in search of a generator. Two heads are better than one, as we had proved surgically on a number of occasions. As always in such cases, we perused *The Torpid Times* for guidance. The headline on that particular day screamed '*Less of the universe than there used to be*'. Powerful, strange sentiments.

What were the odds on that? Still, in my opinion, a little less reality was no bad thing. There was far too much of it. Moving past this oddity, we came to the commercial section. Amongst the usual advertisements for second-hand neutron stars and the like, a large notice caught our eyes.

GENERATOR FOR SALE

MUST BE SOLD

OWNER DISAPPEARING

INVERSE BETTING AGENCY

3.142 LOWER GROTHGRIBBON STREET

Excellent! Just what we needed. I immediately jumped into the horseless carriage, and Morkleberry pulled us to Lower Grothgribbon Street.

The Inverse Betting Agency was a rather odd establishment, located above a pi shop. For a start, it only had a left side. There was no evidence that there had ever been a right side. What should have been the right side was simply an unside. In my ignorance, I had expected to see an establishment with a left *and* a right side, but then I did not get out much these days. Perhaps this was the fashion. We were greeted by the owner, who, like the building, and all of the furniture within, was entirely left-sided. Still, he seemed like a half-decent fellow. He greeted us rather oddly, speaking from the side of his mouth.

'Welc_ _ _. Ni_ _ t_ se_ yo_.'

'Nice to see you too, sir. We have come about the generator.'

'Th_ _ i_ go_ _.'

'Indeed, it is good. How much is the instrument?'

'Ha_ _ a go_ _ ba_. The le_ _ si_ _, plea _ _.'

Half a gold bar? The left side? Or was that half of half of a gold bar? Whichever way, what a steal! Everyone knew that the right side was worth twice as much. Needless to say, we purchased it on the spot, or at least the left side of a spot, which was all there was. Loading it, and my good self, onto the carriage, Morkleberry then proceeded to pull us back to Great Snarkley Street. I must say, he did not do so with good grace. The impudent pup mumbled something about his rights. I pointed out to him that he had far more rights than the poor fellow from whom we purchased the generator. Why, I pulled Sir Snedley around for some three hundred years, and felt honoured every minute!

Arriving at the office, we installed the generator in the main exhibits hall. The machine had a large dial on its front that ranged from minus one to minus one hundred. Curious. Well, I supposed it generated negatively charged currents. That was fine. Time to turn the machine on, and receive the warm regards of a grateful public! I switched it on and the machine began to hum. The needle began to creep up to minus one percent. No power, though. Minus five, still no power. It was then that the oddities began to occur. Or unoccur, to be more accurate. Pieces of reality started to go missing. Important pieces. And still there was no power!

The first indication that anything was awry was when five percent of Morkleberry, specifically his left foot (which still resided on his right side) simply ceased. There one instance, unthere the next. Startled, he hopped gallantly away from the thing. Something was afoot, and it was not only Morkleberry. Still, the numbers kept going up, or down as the case may be. Minus twenty-five, and the front quarter of a particularly lovely goldfish, and its bowl, disappeared. What a loss. Real gold. A real bowl too, as it so happened. Fortunately, the water did not spill out, as there was quite literally nothing for it to fall into. The newly no-front three-quarter fish did not seem too distressed, but then they are rather phlegmatic at the best of times. Fifty percent now, and the left half of all the oxygen molecules in the surrounding space ceased. Reacting quickly, I began to breathe solely with my right lung. We at the Society are trained to react to any eventuality. How extraordinary! I, yes, I Smotheringale, felt that I was losing my mind. And good God, so I was! Half of it was not there. The front half. Galloping stupidity was upon me.

What was happening? Or unhappening? In my desperation, I resorted to thought. Where had we got the thing? The Inverse Betting Agency. Odd name. Odd place as well. No other side. The fellow was pleasant, but not all there, in my opinion. Hmm. Oh, good heavens! This was not an electric generator at all; we had purchased a negative probability generator! It was not that things had a zero chance of being. They were *negatively* likely to exist. They were positively unexisted. Morkleberry had been the first, as he had been nearest the generator. Five percent of the young lad had been negatively likely to exist, and so forcefully hadn't. The higher the numbers got, the more went missing. Worse still, as it powered up, it took things at even greater ranges! At this rate, the universe would *all* be un-universed in next to no time. And *still* no electricity.

What to do? We could reverse the polarity, I mused. I had no idea what that meant, particularly with half my mind having been unbeened, but that is what they say in science fiction. All very well for fiction, but what about the *real* world, where we had a three-quarter goldfish, less of Morkleberry than was considered appropriate, right-sided oxygen, and half my mind lost to unbeing? Tricky. We had to act quickly before we were all unexisted. What could reverse such a thing? I looked at young Morkleberry, his reverse ears twitching, and his inverse legs a quiver (what there was of them). Dear God, there was only one possibility. I would have to brave the Hypercube. This could have unexpected consequences, as Morkleberry could attest to.

I would have to get the angles right, heading ninety degrees into the fourth dimension, and exiting, if at all possible, from a *single* exit. Indeed, the only way I could see it working was if I turned the generator upside down, and walked backwards on my hands through it. I leapt onto my hands, breathing only through my right lung, and bellowed, 'Morkleberry, hop on over and put the generator on my feet.' Taking me literally, and he had little choice given his unipedal status, he hopped over and loaded it on to my upstretched feet, and I marched quickly backward through the nearest entrance.

I will not describe the diabolical dimensional dilemmas I endured. Suffice to say that I exited safely, and all in the one place, at the one time. I quickly checked the dial. Positive. I hastily checked my brain. My mind, author of my greatest services to preposterity, was back! I quickly counted Morkleberry's feet: two. Excellent. And we had a *whole* goldfish. The generator, however, was busy unbeing. It was dealing with the paradox of suddenly being a *positive* negative probability generator. The machine was having an existential crisis. In the end, weighing the positive and negative probabilities, the generator became positive it had a zero chance of existing, and so promptly didn't.

And *still* no electricity!

All in all, a waste of the left half of a gold bar. All appeared well, however, at least until I looked down. Dear God, I had my left foot on frontwards and the right one on backwards. How untidy. I could learn to hate that Hypercube. Extra dimensions matter, they say. So it would seem. How was I to put my best foot forward, even metaphorically? Which one was it, and which way would it go? Still, there is something to be said for a reverse foot. Far preferable to another trip through the Cube. I must say that I could even envisage myself cutting a swathe through a dance floor, a rival to young Morkleberry with his fashionable reverse-leg shuffle. Cutting my toenails, however, could prove tricky.

We had not generated any electricity, and the worldwide blackouts continued. The Society *had*, however, saved the universe from being negatively probabilised. In recognition of this singular achievement, I was presented with the Society Medal for the Negation of Negation, after which I spoke, eloquently and at great length, to an enthralled audience, on *The power of positivity*.

The Perambulations of the Perpetual Irritation Machine

It was Sir Snedley who had purchased the Perpetual Irritation Machine. As he said to me, back in the early years of my second century, 'Smotheringale, we all need a little irritation. While you do your best to provide it, and succeed admirably in most instances, we need something a little more *consistently* irritating.' It was in this spirit that he had purchased a Perpetual Irritation Machine from a certain Professor Beelzebub. A curious fellow. He was a rather lurid vermillion, possessed horns, a tail and wings, and carried a trident. Clearly a man about town.

'It is guaranteed to vaguely irritate all who go near it. In perpetuity, sir!' the Professor claimed.

'The price for this irascible irritant, sir?' Sir Snedley enquired.

'A thousand souls.'

'A thousand soles! Done. You shall have them today.' As Sir Snedley noted to me, the man clearly liked fish. I was duly dispatched to the fish market to obtain this piscine price, and deliver them to the good Professor Beelzebub, who was discussing the perils of atheism with Sir Snedley. I must say he did seem rather astonished when presented with his soles.

'I said a thousand souls, Sir Snedley, a thousand *souls*!'

'And a thousand soles you have, sir. Beautiful, fresh, untainted soles!' While Sir Snedley and I found this conversation somewhat perplexing, we astutely surmised that we were all in furious agreement on the subject.

Professor Beelzebub re-inspected the magnificent ocean harvest, pursed his lips, and remarked, '*Well*, I do rather fancy fish.' We left him frying the soles on his trident, which he must have carried for just such an outcome. From whence the fire came, who could say?

The reader will be well aware that a number of the scientific instruments purchased by the Society over the years have not lived up to their names. Or perhaps they lived up to them a little too well – the tragic case of the Note Taker being a prime example. I still weep for the lost snarkley. The Perpetual Irritation Machine was, however, true to its name. It insisted on being referred to by the aggravating acronym, PIM. It had two main means of creating annoyance to those unfortunate enough to be near it. The first was to create as much disorder as it could. It was rather fond of blending. On one occasion, we were foolish enough to leave our fine, single malt Society whiskey supply in close proximity to a particularly rancid selection of goat's cheese. Quick as a wink, no whiskey, no goat's cheese. Just goat's cheese whiskey. A spritely dram, I must say. While we did spend some considerable time trying to unscramble it, we learnt to like it in the end. It was particularly good on sandwiches.

The PIM also considered being dead more disorderly than being alive, and rightly so. What a disorderly lot the dead are! Walking too close to the PIM, you might suddenly feel your leg go dead. And it would be. Dead a week, at least. The only solution was to hop backwards from the machine and get out of range, have a stiff goat's cheese whiskey, and hope for the best in the Hypercube. If the mood so took it, the PIM was more than capable of doing reverse entropy, undeading the dead, and unwhiskeying your whiskey.

The PIM's second favourite means of annoyance could only be described as a louche literalism or, perhaps, a bombardment of banality. It thrived on actualising metaphor. The more banal the better, and all the more annoying. One fellow recently was heard to utter, perhaps unwisely, 'I have the most awful pins and needles in my legs.' And then, so he had. Both legs absolutely covered in what were truly *awful* pins and needles. The most awful I had seen. There were even a few porcupine quills thrown in for good measure. The fellow was most annoyed. Still, he was better off than the lad with the splitting headache. Worse still, the chap who told us his feet were killing him. Strangulation by foot is a sight not easily forgotten. We at the Society have learnt the value of considered speech.

This was all very well and good, so long as the PIM stayed within the confines of the Society's office. If it were to get out into the larger community, the consequences were likely to be dire. Looking back, it was bound to happen. After all, what could possibly be more annoying?

As with so many of our adventures, it started with an innocent remark by young Morkleberry. He was just passing by the PIM, which promptly blended his ham sandwich with a pottery vase. Looking at his ceramic sandwich, now clearly marked '*Fragile: handle with care*', he commented upon the longevity, and persistence, of the machine.

'My word,' the lad foolishly noted, 'that thing certainly has legs.' Dear God, what was he thinking? Because then, of course, it certainly had. Two particularly strong, athletic legs, with well-turned ankles, clad in the latest running gear. Before he could stop it, PIM was up and running out the front door, off into Great Snarkley Street, and from thence to parts unknown.

The first I knew of this catastrophe was when Morkleberry came racing into my office bellowing, 'Dr Smotheringale, the Perpetual Irritation Machine is on the run!'

How irritating! I stuck my head out of the window, and sure enough, there it was, galloping gracefully down the street. Wasting no time, we raced to the front door, passing by the Tomb of Sir Snedley, our revered founder.

It is worth noting that Sir Snedley's death may, in no small part, be laid at the (now literal) feet of the PIM. One bothersome afternoon, Sir Snedley had felt the need of some music to ease his labours. 'Smotheringale, fetch me an organ grinder.' Having done so, I passed by the PIM. It was, as fate would have it, in one of its literal moods. Upon presenting the organ grinder to Sir Snedley, the PIM lived up to its nomenclature and proceeded to grind Sir Snedley's organs. His last words on this earth (mind you, not his final words) were: 'An absurd death. Excellent! My life is fulfilled.' As always, an example to us all.

Back in the present we were astonished to be met by Sir Snedley himself, newly risen from the dead, and none too pleased about it. Or at least half of him was risen. The top half. Everything from the waist down, however, was decomposing skeleton. The infernal PIM had decided to reverse its usual practice! Knowing what would irritate Sir Snedley the most, who was known to be enjoying his death enormously, it had half undeaded him.

'Smotheringale! Morkleberry! What on earth is going on? There I was, enjoying a well-earned and rather lively death when suddenly I find myself here before you! And only half-dressed! Outrageous!'

'My apologies, Sir Snedley. We have no desire to interrupt your most excellent death. It is the Perpetual Irritation Machine,' I humbly explained. 'It is literally on the run.'

'Good God! Then let us be off after it. There is no time to lose.'

'But how will we know where to look, Sir Snedley?' I enquired.

'Follow the irritation, me lad, follow the irritation!' So saying, off he clattered down Great Snarkley Street on his skeletal legs, hot on the tail of the miscreant PIM.

We knew we were heading the right way when we came to a fork in the road. A pitchfork, to be precise. Some poor fellow was laying under it. He had clearly, rather imprudently, referred metaphorically to a road junction, and the merciless metaphoric PIM had taken him at his word. Further confirmation that we were on the right track came with a sudden localised downpour of cats and dogs. Dear God, why do people speak so loosely about the weather? Most people have not experienced a real feline/canine downpour. For a start, being hit by a falling mastiff is profoundly unpleasant. To make matters worse, the unfortunate beasts tend to explode upon impact with the ground. A slithering forest of entrails. All in all, most unsnairy.

Dodging a downpour of Dobermans, we were hard on the PIM's heels, metaphorically and literally. It had passed by a graveyard, and raised a great number of what had been perfectly happy dead people. More appalling reverse entropy! Like Sir Snedley, they were none too pleased to have their repose interrupted. One old ex-corpse was heard to mutter, 'Life is all very well for the young, but give me a good old-fashioned death any day.' Wise words, I have no doubt. Suddenly, the PIM ran into the Conventional Convention Centre. Excellent. We had it cornered. I looked up at the sign announcing today's conference. The Literary Society was presenting *'The Extended Metaphor in Modern Language'*. Dear God, how appalling! Just then, an extended metaphor came slithering out the door. I do not know if the reader has seen one in the flesh, but it is truly alarming. The PIM was clearly near and at work.

One ill-fated speaker had been opining on '*Home is where the heart is*' as PIM passed by, when suddenly that's where his heart was. Unfortunately, the rest of him wasn't. One can only guess at the reaction of his puzzled family at said home. Naturally, mass panic ensued. The general public is so easily spooked. Just one more reason why we need the cool heads of a Society such as ours! I should not have made this remark to Morkleberry, as suddenly our heads were very cool indeed. Chipping the ice from our heads, we pondered: what to do? It was, of course, Sir Snedley who came up with the solution to our travails. 'We shall lure it with metaphor and banality!' What genius! Dead for years, but still the liveliest mind among us.

'First we must get it out the door.' So saying, Sir Snedley, that canny old knight, approached the PIM and stated quite clearly to it, 'One good turn deserves another!' Of course, we all turned, but so did the PIM. Now facing the door, Sir Snedley leapt upon it, and yelled, 'Hit the road.' The PIM did just that, as did we. Good God, why do they make roads so hard? What a fine sight we made. PIM, Morkleberry and myself out on the road, hitting it repeatedly, and Sir Snedley riding the recalcitrant thing, using his anklebones as spurs. He then cried, 'It's my way or the highway.'

Not even the PIM would disobey Sir Snedley in his ire, and the highway led straight to Great Snarkley

Street in any case. So there we were, on Great Snarkley Street, still hitting the road. Finally, he whispered to it, 'There's no place like home,' a banality of frightening proportions, which totally confused the PIM. If there was no place like home, then home it had to be. And where was the PIM's home? Why the Society office, of course! And suddenly, that's where we were.

Sir Snedley quickly tied the Perpetual Irritation Machine's legs in a triple sheepshank, using a real sheep just to make certain. The ovine omitted a strangled bleat. The gall. You would think that it would be proud to serve.

'That's how it's done, me lads!' he said, as he eased his bones off the PIM.

The reader will not be surprised to learn that this particular adventure ended with a well-deserved awards ceremony. Sir Snedley was posthumously awarded the Society Medal for Entropy Wrangling, which he accepted in person. After giving an excellent five-hour speech entitled '*Dead, the way ahead*', which was warmly received, he retired to his Tomb to enjoy the remainder of his rudely interrupted death. Unfortunately, the others who had been raised from the dead had to endure life until they could re-die and again rest peacefully. I must say that we received quite a number of written complaints about the matter, some from the newly undead, and many more from displeased relatives. The ingratitude of some people!

The Black Hole of Great Snarkley Street

It is difficult to believe that an entire universe can change, possibly for the worse, due to pasta. Yet such has indeed been the case, although most in this universe are unaware of the significance of that calamitous carbohydrate. Would that *we* were. I have also heard it said that some people cannot tell their left from right these days. Well, no wonder! They have been known to wander. This particular wandering began with the wild enthusiasm of young Morkleberry.

The young lad was mad keen to make his own pasta. The sort of absurd, youthful enthusiasm that so many men approaching the end of their first century indulge in. In short, he pestered me until I approved the Society buying a pasta maker. He showed me an advertisement in *The Torpid Times* offering just what he needed.

BLACK HOLE SPAGHETTI MAKER®

SPAGHETTIFIES

ABSOLUTELY

ANYTHING AND EVERYTHING

The price seemed reasonable, so I sent the lad out to purchase the object. He came back some time later carrying a rather small box, his reverse ears quivering with excitement. It certainly did not look like any pasta maker I had seen or heard of.

I took a step forward to look into said box. No easy feat, given my recently reversed foot. Good God, I could see nothing in it! I screwed both monocles in and looked again. Still nothing. The lad had been had. I hoped that he had not purchased another Gap. We needed another one of those like a hole in the universe. Which it was.

'I see nothing but nothing in the box, Morkleberry.'

'It is the nothing that *is* the nothing in the box, Dr Smotheringale.'

There was some sense in that, I thought. *Still.* 'Indeed? Well, it still seems rather small. Are you sure it makes spaghetti?'

'Better than that, Dr Smotheringale. As the advertisement says, it makes spaghetti out of *anything* you put in it! Put anything in one end, and out comes spaghetti from the other.'

'So, what exactly is pasta usually made from?'

'The staple crop is wheat, Dr Smotheringale.'

Wheat? Hmm. Well, we had no staple crop of wheat, but we did have a rather large staple crop of staples where the Attic Ocean had been located. Tricky to grow, but staples are a staple of office life. The secret to a good crop, we found, was to add iron. Lots and lots of it. Indeed, for each staple we used some three tonnes of iron. Expensive, but what fine staples they were! People came from miles around to stand in awe, and say, 'What fine staples, Dr Smotheringale. You certainly have a green thumb.' Which I did. Chartreuse, to be exact.

Fetching some bowls for our dinner, I instructed the lad. 'Morkleberry, fetch a tonne of staples and insert them into the Spaghetti Maker. If we are to make pasta, let us make a goodly amount.'

The lad went off, and came back with freshly cut staples. He immediately started to insert them into the Spaghetti Maker. It was a lot of work, and I would have offered to help, but I was quite busy counting pi backwards by sevens from infinity. A useful exercise that sharpens the mind, and which I would recommend to anyone. Starting was always the problem. As was finishing, now that I come to think of it.

In went the staples and, *whoosh*, we saw them pulled into long strings of spaghetti as they fell in. Excellent! Just what you would expect. But hold on, where was our spaghetti? Shouldn't they come out the other end as beautiful, edible pasta? There we were, standing with our bowls, ready to eat, but nothing was coming out. Come to think of it, where was the other end? I was puzzled. I could have sworn that the box was getting larger.

'Morkleberry, where is my dinner?'

'I do not understand it, Dr Smotheringale. I'll throw some more staples in.'

So saying, he loaded another tonne of staples into the box. Again, I would have helped, but I was cutting the toenails on my backwards foot. A complicated procedure that rattles both the spine and the sense of self-worth. Again, *whoosh*, we watched our spaghettified staples disappear into the box. The thing looked even bigger. Moreover, I was getting the odd feeling that it was pulling *me* towards it!

'I fear, Morkleberry, that we have been sold a pup.'

'No, sir. The man did offer me a young canine, but I explained that Pavlov's Dogs would not approve.' In response, a soggy, salivating serenade emanated from said canines. The Dogs, like Morkleberry, were not strong on metaphor. I rather hoped that Dr Pavlov would return to collect them soon. I understand perfectly that people get delayed, but a hundred years of canine salivation was surely enough to endure.

Most singular, I mused. Singular? And then it hit me, as so many things do. *Black Hole Spaghetti Maker*? Dear God, it was not just a brand name. It actually *was* a black hole! '*Spaghettifies anything*' indeed! It would stretch anything it could reach to pieces, and swallow it up. And it *was* getting bigger. What had the lad done? The only way we could get our dinner would be to wait for the Hawking radiation to dissolve the black hole in around 500 billion years. As the reader will be aware, I am a patient man, but I was hungry.

'Morkleberry!' I bellowed in an electrically charged voice, flustering the lad. He stumbled back in shock, and that was when it happened. He collided with the Insanitiser, tipping *it* into the Hole. Dear God, black holes were difficult enough when they were sane. What on earth would an *insane* black hole do? Would it grab a knife and run amok? Of course not, I reasoned. Black holes don't have hands. They do, however, have hair. I had heard that they have no hair. What nonsense. Of course they do. Black hair. Very stylish black hair.

We did not have to wait long to find out what it would do. The first thing it did was develop a split personality. To our astonishment, there was now a *white* hole in the box as well. It was not sucking anything in. It was spewing things forth. Hello! There were our staples. Still no spaghetti, I noted sadly, my stomach rumbling. I looked closely. My goodness, the left-hand side of the staple was nowhere to be found on the left. It was on the right-hand side! Where was the right side then? Good Lord, there it was on the left! And the whole lot of them were a *good* metre to the left of reality.

The second thing the Spaghetti Maker did was start to pull the entire universe into itself. Such was its Insanitiser-induced grandiosity that it wanted to *be* the universe! Dear God, we had a megalomaniacal black hole with a split personality on our hands that could, potentially, devour the entire universe. Thank goodness the Society was on the case! Looking back, it was extraordinary the number of disasters at which we have happened to be present. A true blessing to the universe.

The first thing we did was put up a sign saying, '*Black hole, do not enter!*' to discourage anyone so minded. This had no effect, as the sign itself went in, disobeying its own advice. Extraordinary. We then put on a rather large, and strong, metal cap to block it. You would think that would work. Gone! We even tried the Great One-Legged One's hoof. *Whoosh*, in it went. Despite our best efforts, everything was speeding up and heading into the Hole. Schrödinger's Clowder, Pavlov's Dogs. The Hypercube! And was that Saturn? It was getting rather crowded in our office. And then, in *we* went, my last word being a stern '*Morkleberry!!!!*'

Was this how Smotheringale was to end? In an irascible, ersatz pasta maker with psychiatric issues? Before we knew it, *we* were being spaghettified. It is an unspeakable experience that I shall now speak of. The first thing that happens is your feet are stretched a long, long way from your head. I looked down. There they were, one facing forward, one back, as usual, but kilometres away from me! Most annoying. I was about to say something to Morkleberry, whose knees were taking a long-awaited holiday from his torso, but as my lower jaw was now a hundred metres from the top jaw, nothing came out.

The next thing that happens is the actual spaghettifying. We were torn into a hundred vertical strips each. There we were, flapping like the spaghetti we were, heading towards the singularity at the centre of the Hole. I was trying to remonstrate with Morkleberry out of the hundred slivers of my mouth, but my teeth were *al dente* by this time and words failed me. Fortunately for the reader, it appears that only those who *know* they are to be spaghettified can remember it. To others it is all a confusing blur that could not possibly have occurred. Readers who were alive at the time will say, 'We remember no such experience, Professor Smotheringale.' No, you wouldn't. In all the cosmos, Morkleberry and I were the only sentient beings expecting it. Although I believe there was a fungal life form from the Andromeda Galaxy who was not entirely surprised. Amongst humanity, however, we alone remember.

Finally, we hit the singularity. Fortunately, there only appeared to be the one. Time stopped completely when we hit it, so we were there for quite a while. Then *whoosh*, out we popped from the white hole! And everything else in the universe came thundering out after us, all settling into place, including Saturn. We waited, cautiously, and gave our hearts five minutes' time off for a well-earned rest. Everything appeared normal. I looked around. And then I saw it. My God! The *entire* universe was a good centimetre to the left of the old reality. How annoying. It was then that I noticed Morkleberry. His reversed legs were reversed! The left was on the left, and the right upon the right! His left backwards ear, however, was on the right, and the right had moved to the left. I look down at my own feet. My left foot on backwards, and the right one on frontwards! *And* I had just gotten used to the old set up.

I looked into the box. The black hole was back to normal size, having emptied the entire universe out, as was our newly acquired white hole. Closing the box, I stated firmly to a disappointed Morkleberry, 'No pasta today.'

Now many will believe this tale to be a work of fiction. Fiction indeed! Not even the most febrile fantasist would, or could, make up such a preposterous tale. Do you not wonder why you frequently have trouble telling left from right? Or drop a glass about a centimetre to the right of where you thought the table was?

We took the box and put it on a shelf with a sign saying, '*Danger! Do not use for pasta making – or anything else.*' Strong, necessary words.

After such an experience, there was nothing for it but to hold an awards ceremony. We had, we can modestly say, saved the universe from itself. In a moving ceremony, I was presented with the Star of Irreversible Reversibility. We all stood a centimetre to the right of ourselves, and the award was pinned on back-to-front, in memory of the old reality.

Sad to say, we never made pasta again.

The Shortest Possible Distance

I was sitting at my desk smoking a ham, cigarettes being deemed passé by Morkleberry and the young crowd. Having an aversion to disease, I insisted to Morkleberry that if I was going to smoke a ham, I would only smoke one that had been cured. I did not enquire of what this particular porcine had been cured. I was engaged upon important Society business, constructing a list of lists, having been engaged by a Dr Google to complete this task. She was a strange woman with a misspelt name, surrounded by a flurry of people constantly bellowing questions at her. I liked the cut of her jib. Why she was wearing one, I had no idea, but it suited her.

'Dr Smotheringale, I require the services of the Society. I am in urgent need of a list,' she informed me.

In all honesty, I could not see why. She had a good fifteen-degree lean to starboard by my reckoning. Still, some like to live on the edge. 'What list would you require, madam?'

'I require a list of lists. A list of every list, past, present and future. All the lists that ever were, are, or will be.'

The request being preposterous, and unarguably absurd, it was agreed that the Society would undertake this important endeavour. The only way to proceed in such instances is with iron logic. Naturally, I commenced the list of lists with the Leaning Tower of Pisa, the Earth, Uranus, and Morkleberry's rather peculiar angle three weeks previously, after the Great One-Legged One trod on him with intent. I had even angled the paper fifteen degrees to vertical in honour of the project and its sponsor. I reached over to my goose for a fresh quill when my hand, instead of grasping that fine fellow, grasped thin air. Hello! Where was my goose? I looked up from my listing to see him sitting on the edge of my desk, some ten metres away. Odd. I screwed in both monocles the better to comprehend this outrage. Good Lord! The goose, and the end of my desk, were now some hundred metres away. The goose and I exchanged astonished glances. I was certain, as was my goose, that my desk was generally, nay always, some two metres long.

'Morkleberry!' I bellowed in a stentorian voice, my own having been muted in astonishment.

'Yes, Doctor?' his voice drifted in from the next room, which appeared to now be some ten kilometres away.

'Get yourself in here, immediately.'

'Certainly, Doctor,' a voice that sounded yet fainter returned. I reached for my telescope. The fellow was now fifty kilometres away, busy polishing the Hypercube. At my command he leapt forward briskly, as only a nonagenarian can, and came running to my office. Some ten hours later he appeared by my desk breathless, exhausted, short of shoe leather, but patently well fed.

'Sorry for the delay, Doctor. I stopped to have morning tea at the Perpetual Irritation Machine, lunch by the Insanitiser, afternoon tea at your office door, and a light supper by your waste bin. The walk was rather longer than I recalled. Have you been renovating?'

Good God! The insouciance! I did not, however, argue with him. Indeed, to keep body and soul on speaking terms during the long wait, I had made the long hike across my desk and helped myself to a decent portion of goose liver pâté. What was happening? While I snacked, and my goose recovered, an ominous idea asserted itself. The Shortest Possible Distance.

'Morkleberry. Where, exactly, is the Shortest Possible Distance? Is it still safely in its box?'

We had come into possession of this remarkable diminutive in Sir Snedley's time, from a certain Dr

Max Planck. He had come to our office, a harried man bearing a substantial, if insubstantial, burden.

'Sir Snedley, I wish to place this, the Shortest Possible Distance, under the Society's protection. I cannot bear the responsibility any longer.'

'My good fellow,' Sir Snedley observed, 'it is passing strange that a man claiming to be in possession of a minimum distance should bear the name of Max. A Max with a Min, if you will.' Sir Snedley was always a man to cut to the nub.

'Indeed, Sir Snedley, it is long-standing family jocularity. The Distance has been in our family's possession for generations. My great, great, great grandfather dug it up while farming potatoes. Recognising it for what it is, he brought it home for safe keeping. Since then, all members of my family have been named Max. Short for Maximum. I have three brothers and two sisters, all Max Plancks.'

'A very sensible move. The saving on vowels alone must be considerable,' Sir Snedley noted approvingly. 'Now, where exactly is this Distance?'

'I have it here in a box.' So saying, Dr Max Planck carefully placed what appeared to be a remarkable nothing upon the table.

Straining to see the object, Sir Snedley enquired, 'Hmm, just how small is this Distance, Dr Planck?'

'Currently, it is 0.000 000 000 000 000 000 000 000 000 000 0001 centimetres. Roughly.'

'And how large is the box it comes in?'

'A trifle larger.'

'Could you not place it in a larger box, which might be easier to find?'

'No, Sir Snedley, if it was in a larger box, we might not find it within the box.'

'Eminently sensible. My eyes are out for dry-cleaning. I believe I will require my monocles.' So saying, the worthy knight donned his monocles. 'Ah, yes, there it is. Most impressive.'

I screwed in my own monocles to observe this phenomenon the better, and there it was. A rather striking shade of ultraviolet catastrophe.

'Now, sir, what exactly does this Distance *do*, besides reside in a slightly larger box?' Sir Snedley enquired.

'It is the most important distance in the known, and unknown, universe. Every distance is a multiple of the Shortest Possible Distance. If it gets bigger, everything is further away. If it gets smaller, everything is closer. One time, it got out of its box and got smaller. There is an old Planck family saying that '*The moon looked so close you could touch it*'. Well, it was, and we did. It must not get out again. We keep a stout lock and key upon the box now.' He then produced an invisible key to the lock, begging us, 'Please take this burden, Sir Snedley, so I may sleep soundly at night.' At the Society, we prefer to sleep quietly, but to each their own.

Having taken on the responsibility, we placed the box and key under the watchful eyes of Cerberus, a three-headed hound we purchased from a Dr Hades. A fine fellow, if a tad lugubrious.

Now, at my question regarding the Distance's location, Morkleberry swallowed uneasily. 'The Shortest Possible Distance, Dr Smotheringale?'

He was looking a little sheepish. In fact, his apparent ovinity made me suspect he had strayed too close to the Perpetual Irritation Machine. I certainly did not remember him having hooves.

'Yes. I seem to recall Cerberus was guarding it.'

'Well, sir, you might also remember that you decided to let Cerberus go. "*Three mouths to feed for a single dog is an unconscionable expense*," I believe you said. We gave it back to Dr Hades, who was well pleased. The class of people entering Hades in Cerberus's absence had declined markedly.'

Ah, yes. Well, under the circumstances, it seemed a worthy sacrifice. After all, we cannot have riffraff entering Hades.

'Well, where is it?'

'I do not know, sir.'

Dear God! Where was the box? No time to lose. We had to find the shortest possible distance to the Shortest Possible Distance. 'Where did you last see it?'

'Near the Hypercube, I think.'

A good 1000-kilometre walk at the current Distance. 'Well, we best get started.' The first day we spent on the trail, we made it halfway to the door of my office. We camped for the evening, and Morkleberry entertained me with a selection of cowboy trail songs. When I say entertained, I am being polite. I glimpsed eternity, and lost the will to live, but felt much better after I removed my eardrums for the night.

After weeks on the trail, we finally spotted the Hypercube in the distance. I suddenly noticed that Morkleberry was standing close to me. Very close indeed. 'Morkleberry, move away please.'

'Easier said than done, sir.'

'Most things are,' I said ruefully. I looked around. My Lord, the Shortest Possible Distance had shrunk. There was nowhere to go. I found this forced intimacy abrasive. As was Morkleberry's beard stubble. Still, that meant the Distance must be close. Then the damnable thing expanded again, and hurtled off into the distance. We trudged on across the weary expanses of our office. We had no choice. Not for the first time, the fate of the universe depended on the Society.

It was Morkleberry who stumbled on it. To be precise, Morkleberry stumbled on it and I stumbled over Morkleberry. What to do? We had to squeeze the Distance back into a respectable size, and get it back into its box.

'Quick, Morkleberry, grab an end. Hold on tight.'

At once, Morkleberry grabbed hold of one end, and your scribe took hold of the other. The Distance, not liking this state of affairs, bucked and writhed under our sturdy grips. It then expanded, leaving Morkleberry some ten kilometres from me. Aware of the urgency of the situation, I immediately sent a carrier pigeon with instructions: *'Push, you scurvy-ridden dog!'* Lest readers erroneously believe I was being impolite to the always enthusiastic and occasionally worthy Morkleberry, my reference was indeed to a scurvy-ridden dog, who had happened to be passing and offered to help.

We were making slow progress. The Distance was stubbornly resisting us every kilometre of the way. We needed to give the Distance a motivation to get back into its box. What could be so awful that life in a box was preferable? There had to be something. Aha!

'Morkleberry, be so kind as to sing. Long and loud. Cowboy yodelling songs, if you will.'

My hands being busy, I stuffed my feet into my ears so as to endure the recital. Taking to the task with enthusiasm, Morkleberry emitted a series of sounds that were enough to shiver the dead. Indeed, a number of respectable corpses came by to complain. All they asked for, they opined, was a quiet death. Indeed, but we had a crisis to deal with. The Distance had never had occasion to be so aurally assaulted. It quivered, it blanched, and began to contract! Excellent. Having the box ready to hand, the very moment it reached 0.000 000 000 000 000 000 000 000 000 000 0001 centimetres, or thereabouts, we pushed it into the box, wrapped it in a stout chain and locked it. It looked somewhat relieved to escape Morkleberry's amelodious assault.

Morkleberry sang on.

'Cease and desist, Morkleberry!' I cried. The universe itself was buckling under the strain of his excruciating onslaught.

I removed my feet from my ears, and reattached them to my legs. The dead retired gratefully to their graves, thanking us for our service and praying they never had to endure such wailing again in their deathtimes. We gave the Distance to Great One-Legged One for safekeeping, with instructions to stomp on it should it ever show its face again.

As one would rightly assume, we held a small awards ceremony. I was honoured to receive the Cross of Universal Distance, after which I made a succinct ten-hour speech that was warmly received by myself and a number of others, living and dead. Morkleberry was awarded the Badge of Aural Absurdity, for crimes against music and sanity above and beyond the call of duty. These were well-earned: once again, the Society had saved the cosmos.

As we basked in our awards, I cast a rheumy eye over the assembly (I had found it on Great Snarkley Street and thought it would come in useful). Young Morkleberry, the Great One-Legged One, the PIM humming away in a most irritating manner. Yes, the future of the Society is in good hands and hoof. Indeed, in possibly four or five hundred years, I may well pass the baton of the Presidency on to Morkleberry. In the meantime, these tales – and others that I deem worthy of recording – will serve to inform preposterity of our ceaseless endeavours. We will always live, die and live, in no fixed order, by the Society's noble motto: *Here to help, hope to hinder*.

Postscript

The reader may now settle back, pour a stiff Liversludge, and reflect in astonishment upon the achievements of the Society. It will by now be obvious to all that the Society has played a major role in preserving the absurd and, indeed, the multiverse. Our universe may well be reversed, and slightly to the left, but it is still here, and you are still here to read about it. Despite our innate modesty, our efforts have not gone unrecognised. Our awards are not given lightly.

It is indeed fortunate that we have so happened to be present when so many catastrophes have occurred. The Ghosts of Gridley Gorge would still be haunting Lady Bloglingdon-Snype's manor if not for our triumphant investigation. Schrödinger's Clowder would be perplexing and annoying the entire cosmos, and the Perpetual Irritation Machine would still be afoot.

The events described in these tales represent, of course, only a small proportion of our deeds. There are many tales still to be told. The Universal Clock, The Wanderings of the White Hole, Sir Snedley and the Sacking of Troy. These tales will be told. I will pluck a fresh quill, skin a calf and prepare a new vellum sheet, screw in my monocles and commit these tales to preposterity.

The universe, indeed the multiverse, rests in safe hands and hoof. Those of the Society for the Preservation of Preposterous Absurdity.

Dr Martin Smotheringale

President

The Society for the Preservation of Preposterous Absurdity

Glossary

Amelodious: An unendurable aural assault upon melody and musical decency.

Ezriquom: One of the lost musical notes. Considered ineffable in its excellence. Beethoven's favourite, as shown in his lost *Symphony in K Ezriquom Major.*

Flozbit: A lost musical note, prized for concertos. A thing of beauty, lost forever.

Hypercube: A four-dimensional cube with an antithetical attitude to reality.

Insanitiser: A device that sucks any remnant shred of sanity from weary brainpans, and replaces it with nonsense.

Morbidinous: Portentously morbid.

Multiverse: More universes than one cares to enumerate.

Necrography: The life of a death.

Negatively probabilised: The unfortunate state of being negatively likely to exist.

Ovinity: The nature of sheepness. Not confined to sheep.

Phantasmagoria: A riotous parade of the absurd.

Preposterity: The preposterous future.

Singularity: An infinitely bent region of spacetime at the centre of a black hole. Infinitely irritating.

Snarkley: A lost musical note, so beloved that Great Snarkley Street bears its name.

Spaghettify: The unfortunate tendency of a black hole to stretch anything to infinity. Not useful for making pasta.

Unsnairy: The best of all possible words. Discovered by Sir Snedley in a disused mineshaft during the Peloponnesian War. Loosely translated as 'unsavoury, awful beyond all comprehension'. More accurately as 'unsnairy'.

Wave function: A probability wave. Not to be confused with a beach party.

Wormhole: A hole between space and time. Not to be confused with lower case 'wormhole', a space between earth and worm.

Acknowledgements

Not all books write themselves. Some do, but this one did not. I would like to thank Joel Naoum for making it possible to unleash the Tales upon an unsuspecting world, Rebecca Hamilton for her excellent editorial input, and Red Tally for the cover art. I also wish to thank Cath Chapman, Jessica Darke, Lilly Darke, Briony Larance and Skye McDonald for their valuable comments on these tales as they emerged from the ether. Finally, I must particularly thank Dr Martin Smotheringale, the true author of this tome.
Shane Darke
Sydney 2019

www.ingramcontent.com/pod-product-compliance
Lightning Source LLC
Chambersburg PA
CBHW030646190726
48286CB00008B/2685